For Tungi, her wonderful family and her dedicated caregivers

First published in 2014 by Child's Play (International) Ltd
Ashworth Road, Bridgemead, Swindon SN5 7YD UK

Published in USA by Child's Play Inc
250 Minot Avenue, Auburn, Maine 04210

Distributed in Australia by Child's Play Australia Pty Ltd
Unit 10/20 Narabang Way, Belrose, NSW 2085

ISBN 978-1-84643-602-4
CLP251013CPL12136024

Printed in Shenzhen, China

1 3 5 7 9 10 8 6 4 2

A catalogue record of this book is available from the British Library

www.childs-play.com

Grandma

Jessica Shepherd

I'm Oscar and I have the best Grandma
in the whole wide world.

We love playing together.
Some days I think Grandma
likes playing more than me!

Sometimes Grandma doesn't feel like playing but we find lots of other things to do together.

We love books. I can even read some to her now.

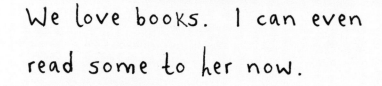

We like to smell the flowers we've just planted...

...and to listen
to the wind chimes
jingle jangle...

...and to wash the dishes
until they shine
like diamonds.

Grandma is always the best at that.

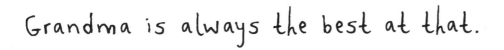

Lately, Grandma is forgetting a lot of things. She nearly missed my birthday!

There are a lot of things she can't do anymore.
I try to help her whenever I can.

Dad says it's important for Grandma to live somewhere where she is safe. She needs to be with people who know how to help her — better than we can.

We will miss her.

Grandma is moving to a special home
where she will get all the care she needs everyday.

I sit in her chair by myself and feel lonely.

Today is the first time I am visiting
Grandma's new home. I'm a bit scared.
But Dad says I can ask as many questions as I like.

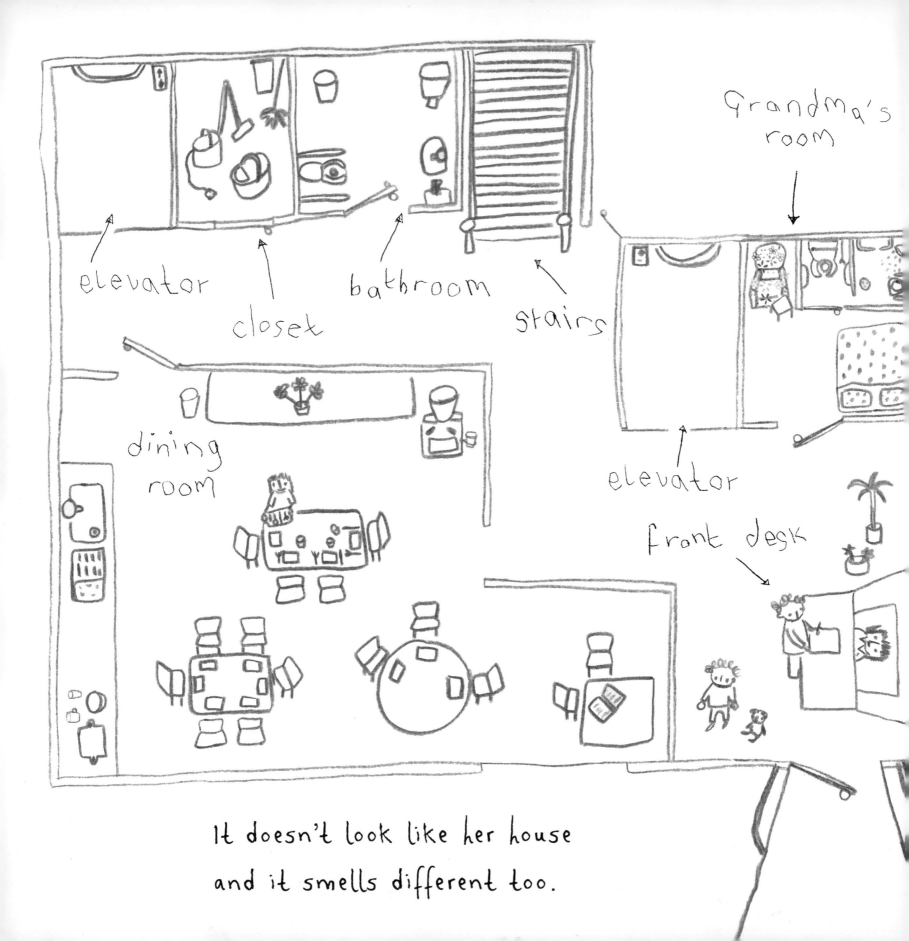

elevator

closet

bathroom

stairs

Grandma's room

dining room

elevator

front desk

It doesn't look like her house
and it smells different too.

Albert's room

yard

day room

There are so many new things
to explore and people to meet.

Grandma is really happy
to see us.

The people who help her are a lot of fun!

And I like her new friend
Albert. He finds a coin
behind my ear.

We have drinks and cupcakes to share.

We usually have cherry, but now and then, Grandma likes chocolate for a change. The caregivers already know that.

Sometimes, Grandma
shouts when people
are trying to help her.
And sometimes, she's
angry with me too,
and I don't know why.

Dad says it's not my fault,
she's just confused.
I know she doesn't mean to be
angry but it still upsets me.

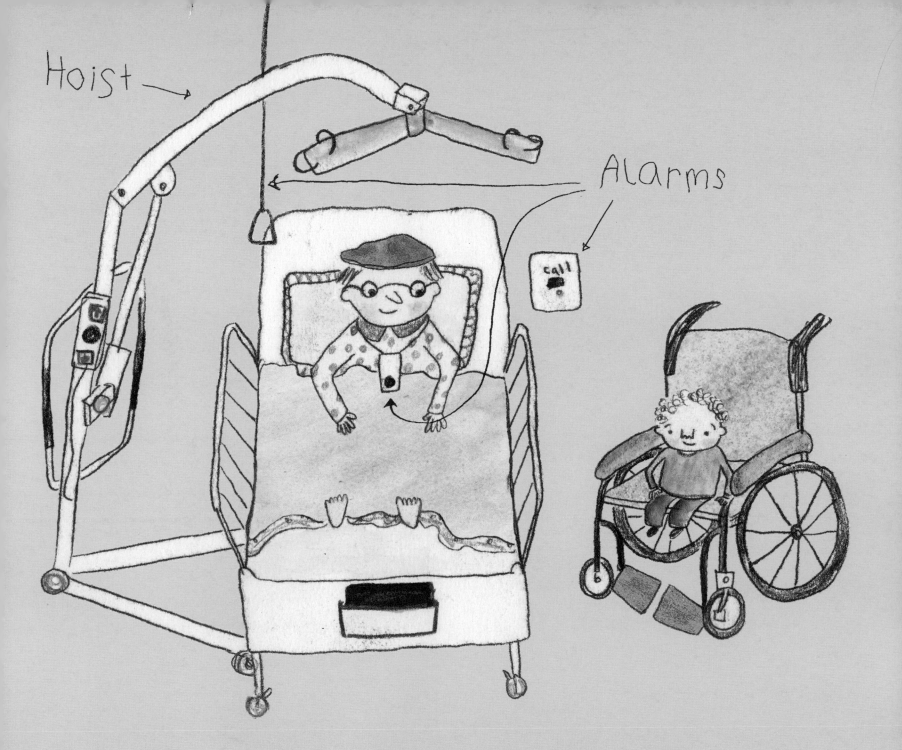

Hoist

Alarms

call

Albert needs help as well.

When his legs won't work, he is lifted with a hoist.

He lets me sit in his wheelchair. I like Albert.

Grandma is getting very forgetful...

...so I made a box of happy memories
that we can look through together.

Grandma still tells me lots of stories about her life.

I know them all by heart, so that
I can remind her if she forgets one day.

Grandma loves it when Dad brushes her long, curly hair.

She still loves dressing up like she did when she was young.

Now that Grandma lives in her new home, we still do lots of things together.

Albert often joins in.

Sometimes Grandma
needs to rest, so
we have quiet times.

It's just nice to be together.

But when Grandma is angry or unhappy
and cannot spend time with me,
it makes me feel sad.

I am lucky because
my friends and family
take care of me.

They are very good at
making me smile again.

It really doesn't matter
whether Grandma is having
a good day or a bad day.

She is still the best Grandma
in the whole wide world.

✳ Let's talk about Grandma ✳

You may know someone who is like Oscar's grandma. Perhaps he or she has dementia and you wonder why. These pages may answer some of your questions and help you to talk about your feelings.

What happens when we get old?

As people get much older their bodies may not work as well as when they were young. When they get ill it can take longer for them to get better.

What is dementia?

People with dementia have a problem with their brain which can cause memory loss and unfamiliar behavior. Alzheimer's is a very common form of dementia. You can't catch dementia. It isn't like a cold or a virus. People can still live well with dementia.

How does dementia change people?

If someone you love has dementia, it can be really hard to understand why they have changed. People with dementia become more forgetful and confused. They have better and worse days. They may make mistakes when doing everyday things, like eating and getting dressed. They find it hard to do simple things that we find easy.

Sometimes, people with dementia get angry and it may seem like they are angry with you. It's usually because they are confused or upset. They might be angry with themselves because they have forgotten how to do something. Imagine how you would feel if you forgot most of what you know!

People with dementia often forget things that have happened recently, but can remember events from a very long time ago. They may remember things about their childhood but not what they had for breakfast. Sometimes they forget things so quickly that they say the same things over and over again. And sometimes they use words we don't recognize. They may forget your name, or not recall who you are. It can be upsetting.

Can I still visit them?

One of the biggest worries is that you never know what to expect when you visit someone who has dementia. Sometimes a visit can be really fun and the time goes fast. Other times it may be really boring and you may just want to go home. It won't always be easy, but a short visit is just as important as a long one.

Can I help?

There are lots of things that you can do with someone who has dementia.

* Talk about things that you have done together in the past. They are still the same person they always were, and they may remember some of these things.

* Make a memory box that contains items you can talk about together, things the person may recognize.

* Share music, it can bring back memories and be really soothing.

* Bring old photo albums you can look through together.

* Make plans. Life doesn't stop for people with dementia. It may be different but it still carries on. Every visit is important. Give them your time.